Enid Blyton's
The Night The Toys
Came To Life

A Templar Book

Produced by Templar Publishing Company Ltd,
Pippbrook Mill, London Road, Dorking, Surrey RH4 1JE.

First published as *The Toys Come to Life* by
The Brockhampton Book Co Ltd 1943.

This edition published 1989 by Gallery Books,
an imprint of W.H. Smith Publishers, Inc.,
112 Madison Avenue, New York, New York 10016.
Reprinted 1990.
Gallery Books are available for bulk purchase for sales
promotions and premium use.
For details write or telephone the Manager of Special Sales,
W.H. Smith Publishers, Inc., 112 Madison Avenue,
New York, New York 10016. (212) 532-6600.

ISBN 0-8317-6396-5

Color separations by Positive Colour Ltd, Maldon, Essex.
Printed and bound by L.E.G.O., Vicenza, Italy.

Enid Blyton's
The Night The Toys Came To Life

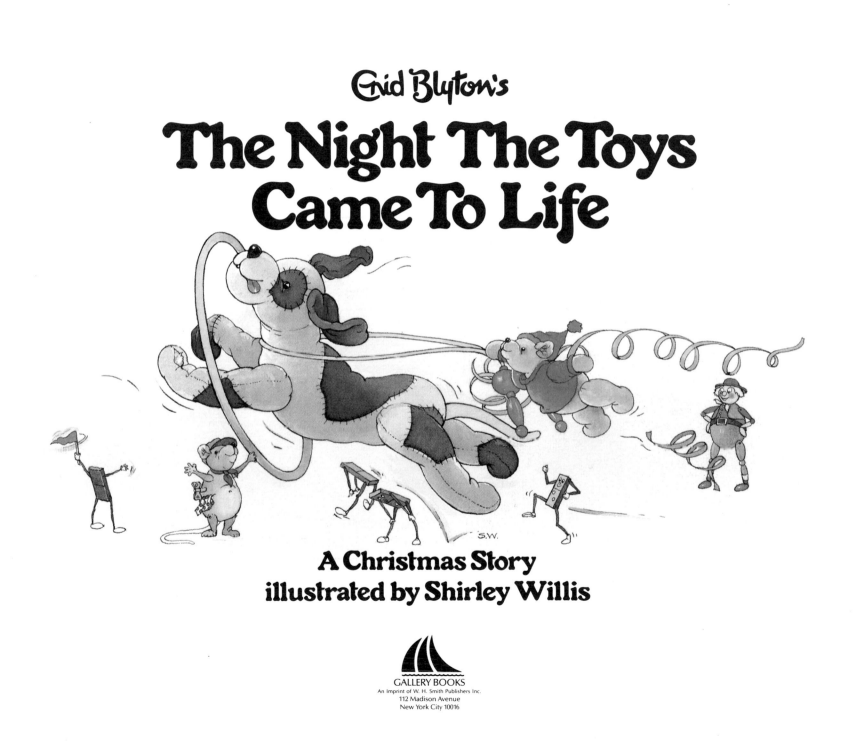

A Christmas Story
illustrated by Shirley Willis

GALLERY BOOKS
An Imprint of W. H. Smith Publishers Inc.
112 Madison Avenue
New York City 10016

It was Christmas Eve and the nursery was very, very quiet. Sarah and Jack had gone to bed. All their toys were shut up safely in the big toy cupboard. Nothing could be heard but the ticking of the cuckoo-clock on the wall.

The cuckoo-bird suddenly popped out of the clock, flapped her wooden wings, and cried "Cuckoo!" twelve times. It was twelve o'clock, the middle of the night.

Now, one toy had been left out of the toy cupboard, just one. It was Teddy, the big brown teddy bear. He had one glass eye, and one boot-button eye. Once he had lost a glass eye, so Sarah had sewn on a button instead, and he said he could see quite well with it. Right now, Teddy was asleep, but the cuckoo woke him up with a jump.

"Who is playing hide-and-seek?" cried Teddy.

The cuckoo laughed and popped her head out of the clock-door again.

"No one," she said. "I was cuckooing twelve o'clock, that's all. Teddy, you have been left out of the cupboard! Put the light on and let all the other toys out, and have a party!"

"Oooh yes!" said Teddy. So up he got, climbed on to a chair and switched on the light. Then he ran across to the toy cupboard. He turned the key – click – and the cupboard door opened!

"Come out, toys, come out!" cried Teddy.

All the toys woke up with a jump. "Who is that calling us?" they cried. "Oh, it's you, Teddy. Can we really come out of the toy cupboard? Oh, what fun!"

Then out came the curly-haired doll, very grand in a pink silk dress. Behind came the small teddy bear with his red hat and red sweater. Then came the jack-in-the-box, the little wind-up mouse, and the wind-up clown, tumbling head-over-heels. Two toy cars came next, and then all the skittles, hopping on tiny legs. The skittle-ball went with them, but he behaved well, and didn't knock the skittles down.

The pink cat and blue dog came together. They were great friends. The wind-up train puffed out, and ran all around the nursery in excitement. And Rag Doll floated down from the top of the cupboard, hanging onto her parasol, so she wouldn't land on the floor with a big bump.

"Hurry, hurry!" said Teddy. "Don't take all night walking out! We want to have some fun, and there won't be very much time."

"What shall we do?" said the curly-haired doll. "Let's do something exciting! Let's have a Christmas party?"

"Oh, yes, yes!" cried all the
toys, and Teddy gave such a shout of
delight that he frightened the
wind-up mouse.

"I'll make some cakes on the
toy stove!" said Teddy. "I'm good
at that." And he started to work.

"Pink Cat and I will go to the toy candy store," said the
blue dog. "There is lots of candy there. We will take some
out of the jars and put them on little plates. Everyone will
like those."

"There is a pitcher of milk on the
table," said the rag doll. "I will get it,
and we will fill the toy tea-pot
with milk, and pretend it is tea."

Rag Doll and Teddy got the pitcher safely down on the floor. The pink cat popped her head into the pitcher and took a lick. "Very nice and creamy," she said. "Oh, Teddy, how delicious your cakes smell! Open the oven door and see if they are nearly ready."

The teddy opened the little oven door, and took out the pan of cakes. They were lovely – warm and brown, smelling most delicious. "They are just ready," called Teddy.

"We had better dress ourselves up for the party," said Jack-in-the-Box. "I shall put on a new hat and polish up my brass buttons a bit."

Everyone hurried to make themselves nice for the party. The curly-haired doll brushed her hair out till it was like a cloud round her face.

·14·

She tied it up
with a blue ribbon.
The pink cat got the blue
dog to tie a fine bow around
her neck, and she tied a blue
bow around the blue dog's tail.
He looked very smart.
    Even the wind-up
mouse got Small Bear to
tie a sash around his fat little
middle. "We want bows, too,"
said the skittles, but there
was no more ribbon left.
"You look quite smart in
your red uniform," said the
wind-up mouse.

"Let's ask the dolls' house dolls too!" said Teddy.
"I am sure they would like to come!" So he knocked at the
front door of the dolls' house, and the little Mother-
doll opened it. She was so pleased when she heard there
was to be a party. "I and Daddy-doll, and all the little
children-dolls would love to come!" she said.

So they all ran out of the dolls' house in their best
dresses and suits, looking as sweet as could be.

"Now we will begin the party," said Teddy. "What shall
we sit on? There are only two dolls' chairs."

"We can each sit on a block!" said the blue dog. "I will

get them out of the block-box." The pink cat helped him to bring out the big wooden blocks, and they set them all around the little table. The curly-haired doll had already put a pretty cloth on it, and had arranged all the cups and saucers and plates from the toy tea-set. She had filled the big tea-pot with milk.

"I want to pour, I want to pour!" said the wind-up mouse. But the doll wouldn't let him. "You would spill the tea," she said. "Go and sit down like a good mouse."

Even the big rocking-horse rocked up to join the party. He chewed up four of Teddy's cakes in no time and he drank fourteen cups of tea – though really it was milk, of course.

"Your cakes are delicious, Teddy!" said the rag doll, and the bear blushed bright red with pride. He looked quite funny for a minute, but he soon became his usual color again. It really was a lovely party.

"Has everyone had enough to eat?" asked Teddy at last. "There isn't anything left – not even a piece of candy, and the tea-pot is empty. What shall we do now?"

"Play games and dance!" cried the blue dog. "Let's play tag! I'll catch you, Small Bear, I'll catch you!" The small teddy bear gave a squeal and ran away. The wind-up clown went head-over-heels as fast as ever he could, and upset all the skittles.

Bang-smack-bang! Down they went with such a noise. The wind-up mouse squealed loudly when one skittle fell on top of him.

"I feel like singing," said the pink cat suddenly. "I want to sing." So she opened her mouth and sang loudly, but nobody liked her song at all. "It's nothing but 'Meow, meow, meow'!" said the curly-haired doll. "Do stop, Pink Cat."

"I want to dance!" cried a big skittle. "We skittles can dance beautifully. We want some music."

"Well, start the music box then," said Teddy.
"I'll wind the handle. Are you ready?" And then
the nursery was suddenly full of loud tinkling music
as the teddy turned the handle of the music box.
What a noise there was!

Now, outside in the street, the night watchman was going on his rounds, with his flashlight in his hand. He was shining it on to people's front-doors to make sure they were closed tight. He was a very good night watchman indeed.

Suddenly he came to a stop. "I hear a strange noise!" he said. "What can it be? It is music playing! It is people squealing and laughing. It is somebody singing a loud Meow song. How very strange in the middle of the night – even if it is the night before Christmas!"

He listened for a little while, and then he made up his mind to find out what all the noise was about. "I am sure the people of the house are all in bed!" he said. "Ho! Who can it be making all this dreadful noise? I must certainly stop it."

Now the toys hadn't heard the night watchman walking by outside, because they were making such a noise. Suddenly they heard a knocking at the window! "Oooh, what's that?" cried Teddy in a fright. "Turn out the light, quickly!"

So the curly-haired doll switched off the light – and then, in at the window shone the night watchman's flashlight. Oh, what a fright the toys got! "Save me, save me!" cried the wind-up mouse and bumped into all the skittles and knocked them down, clitter-clatter, clitter-clatter.

"What's going on here?" said the deep voice of the night watchman, and he climbed in the window. He shone his light all around the nursery. "What, nobody here but toys?" he said in great surprise. "Then what could that noise have been?"

"Please, it was us," said the teddy, in a very small voice. The night watchman was so astonished when he heard the teddy speaking to him that he couldn't say a word.

"You see, we were having a party," said the curly-haired doll, and she switched on the light again. Then the night watchman saw the remains of the party on the table. "Teddy baked some cakes, and the pink cat got some candy from the toy candy store," said the doll.

"Oh, what a pity I didn't come a little sooner," said the big night watchman. "I could have had a cake then. I get so hungry in the middle of the night."

"I'll make you some!" cried Teddy, hurrying to the toy stove. "Have a ride on the rocking-horse while the cakes are baking. They won't take long!"

So the night watchman got on to the rocking-horse, and the horse gave him a fine ride while the cakes were cooking.

The teddy bear baked a beautiful batch of cakes. The pink cat filled a little dish with more candy from the shop. The curly-haired doll tipped up the big pitcher and filled the tea-pot once more. The dolls' house mother-doll took a cup and saucer and plate into the dolls' house and washed it for the night watchman.

Suddenly something happened! The kitchen cat came creeping in at the door, for she had heard all the noise too. She stood there looking at the busy toys – and she suddenly saw the wind-up mouse rushing across the floor!

"A mouse, a mouse!" she mewed, and she pounced on the frightened mouse at once. The mouse's key flew out of his side, and he gave a loud squeal. "Let the mouse go!" cried Teddy. "Bad cat!" shouted the wind-up clown.

But the cat would not let the poor little mouse go. Then the big night watchman got off the rocking-horse and walked over to the cat. He took out his black notebook and a big pencil.

"I must have your name and address," he said to the surprised cat. "I must report you for cruelty to animals. See how you have frightened this poor little mouse!"

The cat fled away in fright. The toys crowded around the night watchman. "Oh, thank you, thank you, kind Night Watchman!" they cried.

"You are so kind," said the clockwork mouse, rubbing his little nose against the night watchman's boots. "I wish you were my very own night watchman. I do like you!"

S.W.

"Come and eat my cakes," said Teddy. The night watchman looked at them. "Dear me!" he said. "I shall never be able to eat all those! Can't we ask someone else to come and share them with me?"

"Let's ask Sarah and Jack!" cried Teddy. "They are asleep, but we can soon wake them."

"You go," said the rag doll. "Tell them we want them to share in our fun. They are nice children and have always been kind to us. It would be fun to share the party with them."

So the teddy went out of the door and tiptoed to the children's room. He climbed up on to the bed and pulled at the sheet. "Wake up," he said, "wake up. There's a party going on!"

Sarah and Jack woke up. They *were* surprised to see Teddy. "Have you come alive?" they said. "Of course I have," said Teddy. "Do hurry up and come to the party!"

So the two children put on their robes and slippers, and went to share the toys' party. They couldn't help feeling very excited.

"Here they come, here they come!" said the toys to one another. "Hello, Sarah; hello, Jack!"

The two children walked into the nursery and were most surprised to see all the toys running around, and the skittles hopping, and the two cars rushing over the carpet.

But they were even more surprised to see the big night watchman. "Good gracious!" said Sarah, staring at him. "What are you doing in our nursery in the middle of the night?"

The night watchman told them. "I heard such a noise in here, and I came to see what the matter was," he said. "Then the toys kindly invited me to their party. But the teddy bear made so many cakes that I knew I couldn't eat them all myself. So he went to get you two."

"Oh, how lovely!" said Sarah. "Teddy, I didn't know you could make cakes. You never said a word about it!"

Teddy bowed low and went very red again. He couldn't help feeling very proud. "Please sit down on the floor," he said, "and I and the dolls will wait on you. It is a great honor to have you and the big night watchman at our party!"

So the two children and the night watchman sat down on the floor, and all the toys waited on them. "Will you have a cup of tea?" asked the curly-haired doll, handing a full cup and saucer to Sarah. "It's really only milk," she said in a whisper.

"It tastes *just* like tea," said Sarah, and she drank out of the tiny cup.

"Will you have one of my cakes?" said Teddy, and offered a plate of his little brown cakes. The children thought they were simply delicious. They crunched them up at once and told the teddy bear that they had never tasted such lovely cakes before. This time Teddy went purple with pride, and the wind-up mouse stared at him in surprise. "Did you know you were purple?" he asked. "You do look funny, Teddy."

The night watchman ate a big meal too – in fact he ate twenty-three of Teddy's cakes, and a whole plate of candy. He drank sixteen cups of tea, which was even more than the rocking-horse had had.

It was a lovely meal, except when the rocking-horse came too near and nibbled some of the night watchman's hair off. That made him rather cross and he took out his notebook again. The rocking-horse was afraid of being asked to give his name and address so he moved away quickly.

"Now what shall we do?" asked Sarah, when they had eaten all the cakes and candy. "We can't very well play games with you toys, because we are rather too big, and we should make such a noise."

"We will give a fine show for you!" said Small Bear. "We will set the music box going, and the curly-haired doll shall dance her best dance. She really does dance beautifully!"

So the curly-haired doll danced her best dance to the music, and everyone clapped their hands. Then the wind-up clown showed how well he could knock down all the skittles by going head-over-heels, but the skittles were tired of that and they chased the clown all around the nursery. He got into the block-box and the skittles locked him in there for almost ten minutes. That made the children laugh.

Then the two cars ran a race with the wind-up train and that was great fun. They all bumped into one another and fell over at the end, so nobody knew who won. Then Small Bear stood on his head and waved his feet in the air. Everybody thought he was very clever. "Can you do that, Night Watchman?" asked Teddy.

"I don't know. I'll try," said the big night watchman, and he got up. But he couldn't do tricks like Small Bear.

He soon sat down again, and mopped his head with a big red handkerchief. "I'd rather watch you do tricks than try them myself," he said. "Hallo – what's this?"

The night watchman and the children saw that the toy farm had suddenly come to life. It stood in a corner of the nursery, and nobody had thought of waking up the farmer, his wife, and animals. But they had heard the noise of the party, and now they were all very lively indeed!

"The ducks are swimming on the pond!" said Sarah.

"The cows are nibbling the toy grass," said Jack.

"The hens are laying little eggs!" said the night watchman in surprise. "And look at those tiny lambs frisking about! There goes the farmer to milk his cows. Well, well, well – it's a wonderful sight to see!"

The toy farm-dog barked around the sheep. The toy horse dragged the toy farm-cart along. The toy pigs grunted and rooted about in their little toy sty. The children really loved watching everything.

"Oh!" said Sarah. "I have always, always wanted our toy farm to come alive – and now it has. Jack, isn't it lovely? Oh, do look – the farmer's wife is offering us a tiny, tiny egg!" So she was. The night watchman and the two children took one each. They were very pleased.

Just as they were all watching the toy farm, a loud noise made everyone jump. It was the toy rooster on the farm, crowing as loudly as he could.

"Cock-a-doodle-doo! Cock-a-doodle-doo!"

"It's day-break!" cried Teddy, in surprise. "How quickly the time has gone."

"It's dawn!" cried the curly-haired doll. "The sun will soon be up. Time for all toys to go back to the cupboard. Hurry now, hurry!

"We must not be alive after day-break. Hurry, toys!"

Then what a hurry-scurry there was for the toy cupboard! The night watchman and the children watched in surprise. The skittles hopped in. The wind-up mouse tore in at top speed. The wind-up clown went head-over-heels right into the back of the cupboard. The pink cat and blue dog ran together, their whiskers touching. Teddy put the blocks into the box quickly. The dolls' house dolls cleared away the party-things, and then ran to their house and shut the front door.

"Good-night – or rather, good-morning!" said Teddy, popping his head out of the cupboard. "So glad you came and shared our fun! Good-bye – and come again another day!"

"Well, that's all over," said Sarah, with a sigh. "Oh, wasn't it fun? Did you enjoy it too, Night Watchman?"

"I should think I did," said the night watchman. "Well, I must be getting back to my work, or somebody will be after me. And you two had better go to bed. I'll get out of the window. Good-night and Merry Christmas!"

"Merry Christmas!" said Sarah and Jack. They watched the night watchman get out of the window and then they went to the nursery door. "Good-night, toys," they said softly.

And out of the toy cupboard came a crowd of tiny voices, from the little growl of Small Bear to the squeak of the wind-up mouse. "Good-night, Sarah and Jack, good-night and Merry Christmas!"

Then Teddy poked his head out of the cupboard again. "It was all because you didn't put me away in the cupboard tonight that the party happened!" he said. "Leave me out again sometime, please!"

"We will!" said the children. What fun they'll have when they do!